For Tim who often goes "looking for adventure"
and sometimes comes home in a cast! – S S

To Laura, Grace and Oscar – L W

Library of Congress Cataloging-in-Publication Data
Smallman, Steve.
Dragon stew / Steve Smallman : illustrations by Lee Wildish.
p. cm.
Summary: When five bored Vikings go looking for adventure,
they decide on a fearless quest to catch a dragon for their stew.
ISBN 978-1-56148-695-3 (hardcover : alk. paper)
[1. Stories in rhyme. 2. Vikings--Fiction. 3. Dragons--Fiction.]
I. Wildish, Lee, ill. II. Title.
PZ8.3.S6358Dr 2010
[E]--dc22
2010004917

Copyright © 2010 by Good Books, Intercourse, PA 17534
International Standard Book Number: 978-1-56148-695-3
Library of Congress Catalog Card Number: 2010004917

Text copyright © Steve Smallman 2010
Illustrations copyright © Lee Wildish 2010
Original edition published in English by Little Tiger Press,
an imprint of Magi Publications, London, England, 2010

LTP/1500/0037/0510 · Printed in Singapore

Steve Smallman Lee Wildish

Dragon Stew

Good Books

Intercourse, PA 17534
800/762-7171
www.GoodBooks.com

Five bored Vikings went out hiking,
   looking for adventure, but what could they do?
"Let's have a battle," said Grim, "or steal some cattle!"

But the other Vikings said,

"Well, THAT'S nothing new!"

Boring!

"Let's go fishing in the dark for a massive, monster shark!" suggested Bushi Bigbeard, but Harald hollered, "Poo!

"Let's wrestle with a bear in just our underwear!"

But the other Vikings said,

"Well, THAT'S nothing new!"

"I'm really bored with hiking!" moaned Yop,
the grumpy Viking.
Then little Loggi Longsocks said,
"I know what we'll do.
We'll go and catch a dragon,
then tie it to a wagon,
then take it home and chop it
up and make a dragon stew!"

So they picked up the wagon that they needed for the dragon,
a stack of sardine sandwiches in case they missed their tea,
a fishing net, a ball of string, a pointy dragon poking thing—
and stuffed them in a longboat and rowed it out to sea.

They sailed away together
through stormy winds and weather,
till a squelchy squeezy squid came
looking for a fight.

But one whiff of Harald's sock and the squid collapsed in shock.

And in no time all its tentacles were tied up good and tight.

I'm knot amused...

They traveled on and on
till all the sandwiches were gone.
But where was Dragon Island?
They didn't have a clue!

Then Bushi grabbed the tail of a passing killer whale and said, "Take us to the dragon or we'll make a stew of YOU!"

OKAY!

ive happy Vikings went out hiking on a fearless quest to catch a dragon for their stew.

They tiptoed over logs and they splashed through squelchy bogs,

till they came across a gleaming,
steaming pile of . . .

DRAGON POO!

They hurried on until
they saw a knobbly, bobbly hill.
"Let's climb it!" Loggi Longsocks said.
"We'll get a better view!"
"Are we there yet?" grumbled Yop
as they struggled to the top.

Then they shouted all together:
"OI, DRAGON, WHERE ARE YOU?"

"Visitors, how sweet! Now would you like something to eat?"

"YES!" cried the Vikings.

"FRESH DRAGON STEW!"

Get him!

Then they started to attack him
and to poke him and to whack him.
And the dragon said,
"Oh, really, what a NASTY
thing to do!"

The dragon twitched his snout
and a jet of flame shot out.
It burst behind the Vikings
and set their pants alight!

Harald hollered, "MOM!"
and Grim said, "OOH, ME BUM!"
And they legged it to their longboat
with their bottoms burning bright.

ive sore Vikings all quite liking
cooling off their bottoms in the sea so blue.
Harald said, "We're lucky—dragon probably tastes yucky!"

Then Bushi roared, "I'm really bored!

SO, NOW WHAT CAN WE DO?"